The Boxcar Children® Mysteries

THE MYSTERY ON BLIZZARD MOUNTAIN

created by
GERTRUDE CHANDLER WARNER

Illustrated by Hodges Soileau

ALBERT WHITMAN & Company
Morton Grove, Illinois

Library of Congress Cataloging-in-Publication Data

Warner, Gertrude Chandler, 1890-1979
The mystery on Blizzard Mountain/
created by Gertrude Chandler Warner;
illustrated by Hodges Soileau.
p. cm. — (The boxcar children mysteries)
Summary: When the Alden children go camping on Blizzard Mountain,
a place said to be inhabited by a ghost looking for buried treasure,
they begin to think someone or something is trying to scare them off.
ISBN 0-8075-5493-6 (hardcover)
ISBN 0-8075-5494-4 (paperback)
[1. Ghosts—Fiction. 2. Buried Treasure—Fiction. 3. Mountains—Fiction.
4. Brothers and sisters—Fiction. 5. Orphans—Fiction.
6. Mystery and detective stories.]
I. Soileau, Hodges, ill. II. Title.
III. Series: Warner, Gertrude Chandler, 1890-
Boxcar children mysteries.
PZ7.W244 Mxqu 2001   2001045672
[Fic]—dc21   CIP

Copyright © 2002 by Albert Whitman & Company.
Published in 2002 by Albert Whitman & Company,
6340 Oakton Street, Morton Grove, Illinois 60053.
Published simultaneously in Canada by
Fitzhenry & Whiteside, Markham, Ontario.
10 9 8 7 6 5 4 3

Cover art by David Cunningham.

Contents

CHAPTER 1

A Mountain of Surprise

"Left. No! No, turn right," said fourteen-year-old Henry Alden. He held the map up and frowned. "Yes, that's it. We're supposed to turn right at the next stop sign."

James Alden nodded. He was Henry's grandfather, and he was driving his four grandchildren — Henry, Jessie, Violet, and Benny — to visit the daughter of an old friend. Her name was Maris Greyson and she was a park ranger at Seven Mountains Wilderness Park.

"Are we lost?" Violet, who was ten years old, asked in a worried voice. "We've been driving for a long, *long* time."

"We're not lost," Henry said cheerfully. "We'll be there soon."

Six-year-old Benny, who had been looking out the window, said, "We haven't passed any houses for miles and miles."

"Oh — but look," twelve-year-old Jessie said. "There's a sign that says 'Greyson.' "

Grandfather turned down a very narrow, very bumpy dirt road. They rocked from one rut in the road to another.

Finally, Grandfather stopped the car in a small clearing. In the middle of the clearing was a small log cabin. The door opened and a big, furry dog came bounding out.

A woman followed the dog out into the clearing. "Shoe," she said, "heel!" The woman was small and strong-looking, with short jet-black hair. She wore jeans, hiking boots, and a red-and-black-checked wool shirt.

Grandfather got out of the car. "Maris

Greyson, it's good to see you," he said. "It's been much too long."

"It has," she said with a quick smile. "But you haven't changed." She gave Grandfather Alden a hug. "It's so good to see you, James. Welcome to Seven Mountains Park."

"Is your dog nice?" Benny asked, almost tumbling out of the car. "We have a dog, but we didn't bring him. We found him when we were living in the boxcar. His name is Watch and he's a good watchdog."

"Whoa, Benny. Slow down," said Henry. He put his hand on his brother's shoulder.

"My dog's name is Snowshoe, Shoe for short, and she's friendly to people," Maris said.

"May we pet her?" Violet asked.

"Sure," said Maris. "Shoe, come!"

"Hey there, Shoe," said Henry, bending to stroke the dog's back. "She looks almost like a wolf."

"Husky, mostly, with a few other things thrown in," said Maris. "I found her wandering on one of the trails when she was still practically a puppy. She was a skinny little thing. You wouldn't know that now, would you, Shoe?"

The dog's ears flattened when she heard her name and she wagged her tail harder.

"These are my grandchildren," said Grandfather. "Henry, Jessie, Violet, and Benny."

"Pleased to meet you. Come on in," said Maris. "I'm making stew for dinner. I'll show you where to put your gear. By the time you unpack, it'll be time to eat."

"Henry and I can unload the car," Jessie volunteered. Jessie liked to take charge and organize things.

In a few minutes, Henry and Benny were climbing up a ladder to a sleeping loft at one end of the cabin, pulling their packs and suitcases behind them.

"Wow," said Henry. "This is cool." He looked around the loft, tucked under one end of the sloping roof. Two narrow beds were pushed against each wall. A skylight let in the last rays of the sun above them.

"I like it here," Benny said. He began to unpack.

"Me, too," agreed Henry, doing the same.

At the other end of the cabin, Violet and Jessie were unpacking in a loft that looked just like the boys'. Down below, they could hear Maris talking to Grandfather as he unpacked his things. The good smell of stew filled the cabin.

"I'm hungry," Benny said suddenly. He leaned over the railing that enclosed the loft and sniffed. "Very hungry."

"Me, too," called Jessie from the other loft.

"Come on down," Maris said, looking up at them. "As soon as the table is set, we can eat."

Benny scrambled down the ladder in a flash and soon all four Alden children had the table set.

They ate hungrily. Soon they'd cleaned their plates and started on second helpings. The mountain air had made them all hungry.

"I like this cabin," said Jessie. "It's sort of like living in the boxcar."

The Aldens told Maris the story of how they had become orphans and gone to live in an abandoned boxcar in the woods. They hadn't known that their grandfather was looking for them and wanted them to come live with him.

"Then he found us and we live in Greenfield now," Violet said. "Grandfather put the boxcar in the backyard and we can visit it whenever we want."

"An amazing story," said Maris. "And now I know what to do if I ever need more room in my cabin. I'll just get a boxcar!"

Benny suddenly yawned. He covered his mouth. "Excuse me," he said.

"We should all go to bed early tonight," Grandfather said.

"I'm not sleepy," Benny insisted. But his eyes drooped.

"Going to bed early is a good idea," said Maris. "Because when you get up in the morning, I'm going to have a surprise for you."

Benny sat up. His drooping eyelids opened wide. "What is it?" he asked. "Is it a mystery? We're good at solving mysteries."

"There *are* a few mysteries in these mountains, but that's not the surprise," said Maris.

"What kind of mysteries?" asked Henry. He and the others forgot about the surprise for a minute.

"Well, the most famous mystery is the mystery of Stagecoach George," Maris said.

"Who is Stagecoach George?" asked Jessie.

"Once upon a time, about a hundred years ago, or maybe more, a very unlucky bandit named Stagecoach George robbed the local stagecoach. It was carrying a big strongbox full of gold to the bank. He got the loot, made his escape, and headed for what is now Blizzard Gap. He knew no one could catch him in these wild mountains.

"But Stagecoach George never had any luck that wasn't bad," Maris went on. "He got halfway up Blizzard Mountain — that's the tallest and wildest of these mountains — and the snow started falling. His horse was getting tired, too. So George decided to bury the loot and come back for it later.

"He'd just finished hiding the loot when his horse went crazy on him. The horse snorted and reared and then it jerked the reins free from George's hand and tore off down the mountain."

"Oh, no," breathed softhearted Violet. "Poor Stagecoach George!"

"That's when he heard an awful roar up the mountain above him, like a thousand trains thundering down the track with a thousand tornadoes right behind them."

"Uh-oh," Benny said. "I bet I know what that was!"

"Right," Maris said. "And George knew just what it was, too. It was an avalanche. He jumped just like his horse had done — for it had known something was wrong, the way animals do. Anyway, George jumped and tried to run, but it was too late."

"And that was the end of Stagecoach George?" asked Henry.

"Yep," Maris said. She leaned back. "Except some people claim they've seen his ghost. They say it's guarding his treasure, trying to figure out a way to dig it up and take it off the mountain."

"Wow," said Jessie. "That's a great story. Maybe we can find the treasure!"

"Or the ghost," said Benny.

"No such thing as a ghost," Grandfather reminded them. "But it *is* a good story."

"And there might be such a thing as treasure buried by the avalanche," Maris said. She shook her head. "At least, some people still think so."

"Can we go look for the treasure on Blizzard Mountain?" Benny asked.

"Hmmm. We *might* be able to arrange a trip to the mountain," Maris said. "Now who wants dessert?"

"Just a little," said Benny.

Everyone laughed and Benny grinned. He never said no to dessert.

Benny went to bed with his head full of stagecoach robbers and surprises. He was sure he would never be able to fall asleep.

But the minute he closed his eyes, he fell into such a deep sleep that he didn't even notice his brother climbing up into the loft or hear Henry say softly, "Night, Benny," before he, too, got into bed and fell asleep.

Jessie fell asleep right away, too. But Violet lay awake for a little while longer. She thought about stagecoach robbers and avalanches and ghosts. Once, she thought she heard a sound outside the cabin. She peered through the narrow window by her bed, but she couldn't see anything except how very, very dark it was.

CHAPTER 2

Lost Treasure

"What's the surprise?" Benny demanded first thing the next morning.

Maris slid a plate of pancakes in front of Benny and said, "It's a camping trip."

"A camping trip! I like camping," said Benny.

"I need to do a little trail scouting on Blizzard Mountain for a couple of days and I wondered if you would like to come along," Maris said.

"Blizzard Mountain? That's where the treasure is!" Benny cried.

"Yes!" said Jessie. "We'd love to come along!"

But Violet had a question. "What's trail scouting?" she asked.

"Well, here in Seven Mountains Park, we try to close trails that are getting worn out by too many hikers and climbers," Maris explained. "They're not as safe, and it's hard on the land around the trails, too. So we give the trails and the land a rest, and work on rebuilding the trails and making them safe again."

"That's a good idea," said Henry.

Maris nodded and smiled and went on, "We're closing the Annie Oakley Trail on the east side of Giant Mountain at the end of this season, and we're going to open a new trail on Blizzard Mountain. Part of my job is to hike Blizzard Mountain and mark the best way for the trail to go. We've already started work on it, but we have lots more work to do."

"Trailblazing," said Henry. "We'll be trailblazers."

"Let's go," said Benny. "I'm done with breakfast."

Maris laughed. "Not so fast, Benny," she said. "We've got a few things we need to do first to get ready. We need to pack. And we'll have to stop in Blizzard Gap to get some gear and supplies," Maris said.

"Are you coming with us, Grandfather?" asked Violet.

But Grandfather shook his head. "No. I'll stay here with Shoe. We can do a little hiking around the cabin."

"Wouldn't you rather be an explorer?" Benny asked.

"You go explore, Benny," Grandfather said. He laughed. "Who knows? Maybe you'll even find the treasure."

"Yes, we will," said Benny confidently. He didn't mind when Maris laughed. He was sure that a mystery was waiting for the Aldens up on Blizzard Mountain.

A little while later, Henry had tossed the last backpack into the back of Maris's truck, on top of all the other camping gear he and Jessie had loaded. "That's the last of it," he said.

"We're ready to go, then," said Maris.

The children climbed into the truck. It was a tight fit. They waved good-bye to Grandfather and Snowshoe.

Then Maris turned the key in the ignition.

Nothing happened. She tried again. *Click, click* went the key. But the truck wouldn't start. Maris frowned. "What is wrong with this truck? I just did some work on it." She got out and opened the hood of the truck and peered inside. Grandfather came to join her.

"Oh, no. It might be the battery," Maris said. She got back in the truck again and turned the key. Still nothing.

"You're right, Maris," Grandfather said. "It must be the battery."

With a sigh, Maris got out of the truck. "That's the second time in two weeks!" she said. She put her hands on her hips and frowned at the battered red pickup truck. "I don't believe this! I'll go call Carola Gallo for help. She's my closest neighbor."

Soon an old blue van came bouncing down the dirt road that led to Maris's cabin.

A tall woman with a wiry build and thick blond and gray hair got out.

"Thanks for coming," Maris said. "Sorry to call so early."

"I'm always up early," Carola said crisply. "And I have an appointment over in the county seat today anyway. You're right on the way."

Maris introduced all the Aldens. Carola gave them a quick nod. She said to Maris, "Battery again? Maybe it's time for a new truck."

"Ha," said Maris. Carola got some jumper cables and attached them to her truck's battery and the battery of Maris's truck.

Maris got in her red truck and turned the key. Her truck started.

"It's fixed! Now we can go to Blizzard Mountain!" said Benny.

"Blizzard Mountain?" Carola asked.

"We're going to help Maris start work on a new trail," Jessie explained.

"I told you, remember?" Maris reminded her.

Carola raised her eyebrows. "So soon after those bear sightings, Maris? Do you think that's safe?" she asked.

"Carola, you're the only person who's reported bear sightings," Maris reminded her. "And we all know you don't want any people on Blizzard Mountain."

"No people? Why not?" Henry asked.

Carola shook her head, frowning fiercely. "That's not true! I just think we need to limit the number of people who use it every year. That protects the animals and where they live. Too many people tear up a park. In fact, too many people make it more like, well, a city."

"Every time we open a new trail, it's only because we've closed another one. You know that," Maris said.

"We should be closing more trails and *not* opening new trails at all. There are too many trails as it is," Carola argued.

Maris started to speak, but Carola kept talking. "If people want to go off the trails, they can hire guides to show them the way. Guides will make sure that they take care of the forest. And that they don't get lost!"

"If we put a real trail on Blizzard Mountain, at least we won't have to rescue lost hikers up there so much," said Maris with a smile.

"Hmmph," said Carola. "If you're hiking on Blizzard Mountain, I'd watch out for bears."

Carola climbed back into her van, slammed the door, leaned out the window, and added, "And just for the record — I'm more worried about the bears than I am about you." She drove away in a cloud of dust.

"Wow," said Benny. "I don't think she likes us."

"She's got a quick temper," Maris admitted. "And she loves these mountains more than she likes most people."

"Did she really see bears on Blizzard Mountain?" asked Violet.

"If she did, she's the only one. The bears avoid the people around here. If you see a bear, it's usually because it didn't see you first and have a chance to run away," Maris said. "I know I haven't seen any fresh sign of a bear near the trail. No tree markings."

"Tree markings? What are those?" asked Benny.

"Those are places where bears sharpened their claws or pulled dead trees and logs apart looking for insects. Insects and berries are a big part of a bear's diet," Maris told him.

"Insects. Yuck," said Violet, wrinkling her nose.

"It's funny that Carola forgot I was headed up to Blizzard Mountain today," Maris said. "We talked about it just a couple of days ago, when she reported the bear sightings. Oh, well, let's get started."

Once more, the Aldens and Maris piled into the truck.

"Is Blizzard Gap far?" asked Benny as they drove away.

"Not too far," Maris answered. "But we have to make another stop first."

"Where?" Violet wanted to know.

"To get Bobcat," Maris said.

"A bobcat!" Violet gasped.

CHAPTER 3

No Such Thing as Ghosts

"Not a real bobcat, Violet," Maris reassured her. "Bobcat. Bob Leeds. Everyone calls him Bobcat. He's a park ranger and an expert on bobcats, too. That's why he's called Bobcat," Maris said.

She turned down a long, bumpy road, which led to a stone house not much bigger than Maris's cabin. A round man with round glasses came out. He waved, closed the door of his cabin, and lifted a large backpack from the porch. He walked to the back of Maris's truck and tossed the pack in.

Then he came around to join the Aldens and Maris.

"Hi there. I heard you were coming," said Bobcat with a grin.

"I like your hat," Jessie said. It had a paw-print design on the front. "Is that a bobcat track on it?"

"Yep," he said. "Not actual size, of course."

"How big is a bobcat?" asked Violet.

"Oh, the average is about the size of a medium-to-small dog," he told them.

"And they don't eat people?" Violet asked, just to make sure.

"Nope. Too small. They're also very shy. My job is to gather more information on them so we'll be able to do a better job of protecting them."

"Protecting them? From bears?" asked Benny.

"People, mostly," Bobcat answered.

"Don't you want trails in the park, either?" asked Jessie. "Are you like Carola?"

"I agree with Carola and I disagree with her," Bobcat said. "The park belongs to everybody, but that means that everybody has to help take care of it, too. Part of taking care of it is staying on the trails and not tramping through important habitat."

"What's a habit . . . habit . . . ?" Benny asked. He'd never heard that word before.

"Habitat," Bobcat repeated. "All it means is home. Where the animals live. You could say that your hometown is your habitat, Benny. And I guess you wouldn't much like it if someone took a walk right through your front door."

"No way!" said Benny.

"Well, neither would a bobcat. So part of my job is to make sure park trails don't go through a bobcat's front door, either."

Just then, Maris slowed the truck down. "Blizzard Gap," she announced. "This is Main Street."

Blizzard Gap was much smaller than Greenfield. Maris drove by a gas station with a sign that said LULU'S GAS 'N' GO, a building with a general store on one side and a diner on the other, and a neat white house with a post office sign out front.

Above the general store, a sign advertised GROCERIES AND EVERYTHING ELSE.

Maris parked in front of the diner.

"Why don't you kids get some hot chocolate in the diner while Bobcat and I get some camping supplies at the general store," Maris said.

"Okay," said Benny cheerfully. "I like hot chocolate."

As the Aldens walked into the diner, people turned to look at them. Violet blushed a little. She was shy.

But Benny smiled at everyone. "Hi," he said. He even waved at a man with curly black hair as they passed his table on the way to the counter.

The man looked surprised. "Hello," he said in a gruff voice. He smiled a little. His teeth were big and white against his beard.

A tall, thin waitress with silver hair came over to take their order. The name embroidered on her shirt said RAYANNE.

"Menu's on the wall," Rayanne said. She nodded toward a big blackboard at the back

of the diner. "Regular items on the left, specials on the right."

"Hot chocolate, please," said Benny. The others ordered hot chocolate, too.

"And I don't suppose you would want whipped cream with it?" Rayanne asked.

"Yes! Please!" Benny said loudly.

One side of the waitress's mouth turned up a little and her eyes crinkled in amusement. "I'll see what I can do," she said.

Henry took a map out of his jacket pocket. He unfolded it and spread it on the counter so Benny, Jessie, and Violet could see it. "Here's where we are now," he said. "And here's where Maris's cabin is."

"There's Blizzard Mountain," Violet said. "That's where we're going."

"If we don't have any more bad luck today," agreed Jessie.

Henry frowned. "I sort of wonder if someone didn't make that bad luck for Maris," he said in a low voice.

"What do you mean, Henry?" asked Violet.

"Carola made it pretty clear she doesn't

want anyone building new trails. Maybe she's been fixing Maris's truck so it wouldn't start, to try to discourage her," Henry said.

"It didn't work," Violet pointed out.

"No. We're still headed for Blizzard Mountain," Jessie said.

"And she helped fix Maris's truck both times," Benny said.

Just then, Rayanne returned with their drinks.

"Blizzard Mountain?" asked Rayanne as she set the four cups of hot chocolate in front of the Aldens. "You kids headed up that old mountain?"

"Yes," said Henry.

"I hear it's a bad luck mountain," said Rayanne. "Haunted, too."

"We know all about Stagecoach George," said Jessie. "We're not afraid of ghosts."

The man with black hair spoke up from the next table. "I wasn't afraid of ghosts, either, until this happened," he said. He leaned over and thumped his leg. "It broke my ankle for me."

"Ah, Chuck, everybody knows you saw your shadow and thought it was a ghost and that's how you broke your ankle," one of the other waitresses teased.

"Ha-ha," Chuck retorted. "I know what I saw up on that mountain. I say if it looks like a ghost and sounds like a ghost, it's a ghost."

"You saw the ghost of Stagecoach George?" Benny said. He almost spilled his hot chocolate, he was so excited.

"That's right, young man," Chuck said. He flashed his teeth in another big smile. "That's what made me fall down the mountain and break my ankle."

"Stop telling tall tales, Chuck Larson," Rayanne said. "You know there's no such thing as a ghost. And you a history teacher!"

"That's how I know so much about it," Chuck said. "It's a history teacher's job to know the history of a place he's visiting. And Stagecoach George is known to haunt Blizzard Mountain."

As Chuck finished speaking, Bobcat came in and sat down next to Benny.

"Mr. Larson says he saw the ghost of Stagecoach George," Benny reported excitedly.

"I know," said Bobcat. "I was part of the group that rescued Chuck. A hiker found him and got us, and we carried him down off the mountain. Chuck told us and everybody else to stay off Blizzard Mountain because he'd seen a ghost."

Jessie turned toward Chuck Larson's table. "If you saw Stagecoach George's ghost, you must have been near the treasure, right?" she asked Chuck.

"I don't know about that," Chuck said. "I think the ghost is still looking for the treasure, not guarding it. He doesn't want anyone to find it before him, so he haunts the whole mountain. But you know what else I think?"

Rayanne rolled her eyes. "*Of course* I know what you think. You think that the avalanche swept the stagecoach gold down the mountain and it's somewhere near the bottom and the ghost is haunting the wrong place," she said.

Chuck blushed a little. "I guess I've said it all before. It's been a few months now. But I'll never forget seeing that ghost. White and misty and floating through the trees," Chuck said. "And howling. When it started to howl, that's when I tripped and broke my ankle."

Bobcat said, "You're lucky that hiker found you when he did. You could have been stuck up on the mountain for a long time."

Again Chuck's teeth flashed in a smile. "I got pretty lost. I thought I was hiking up Pam's Peak. I guess I'm not much of a woodsman."

"If it's been so long since you broke your ankle, why are you still on crutches?" Jessie asked.

"I stumbled and reinjured it, that's all," Chuck said. "But now even a busted ankle can't keep me away from these mountains. I'm doing a history project on Blizzard Gap and this park. And according to my re-search, it has been a bad luck mountain ever since Stagecoach George. Look at everything that's happened up there. Floods. Lost hikers. Rock slides."

"There hasn't been an avalanche in these mountains in over sixty years," Rayanne said. "And floods happen all over these parts when the spring snow melts and it rains."

"How do you know that?" asked Bobcat. "You must like these mountains better than you think, to know all that about 'em, especially since you've only been here since the summer."

Rayanne shrugged. "I'm not a big hiker, but the mountains are pretty to look at," she said.

Chuck stood up and reached for a pair of crutches propped on a chair next to him. His chair fell over with a crash. When Chuck made a grab for the chair, he overturned the sugar bowl. Packets of sugar slid across the table.

Jessie jumped up and righted the chair. Then she put the sugar packets back in the bowl.

"Thanks," said Chuck. Then he began to limp awkwardly toward the bathroom in the hall between the restaurant and the general store.

"If you ask me, he broke his ankle just being plain clumsy," said Bobcat.

"Ghosts. Bad luck. Phooey," said Maris, who'd just come in. "The only reason people still talk about that old story is because nothing ever happens in Blizzard Gap. The last big crime around here was when someone painted the doors of the firehouse blue!"

"No, it wasn't," Rayanne said suddenly.

Everyone looked at Rayanne. She said, "Remember the burglary at the Seven Mountains Museum over in the county seat?"

Maris said, "How did you know about the robbery, Rayanne? You didn't move to Blizzard Gap until after it happened."

"Heard about it," Rayanne said. "All the news in town goes through this diner and a waitress is just naturally going to hear most of it."

"Folks around here are saying it was the work of professionals," said Bobcat. "I mean, look at what the robbers took. Gold bricks. You have to plan a robbery to haul away gold bricks. They're heavy!"

"The museum didn't have much security," remarked Rayanne. "It couldn't have been such a hard place to break into. They say there was no sign of a break-in."

"Doesn't that just prove the burglars were professionals?" asked Chuck, who'd come back in and settled again at his table. "Probably a whole gang of thieves. From a big city somewhere."

"What else did the robbers take?" asked Henry.

"Nothing else except a purple velvet cape. But it was historically priceless," said Rayanne. "It was worn by Jenny Lind, a famous singer who visited the town once. She left her cape behind with the owner of the old opera house as a memento."

"Maybe that's what the robber used to escape!" said Chuck, and several people snickered. "Put on the velvet cape and flew away." Chuck flapped his arms, enjoying the audience.

Maris rolled her eyes. "Time to go," she said to the Aldens and Bobcat. They finished their hot chocolate and got up to go.

"Let's not forget the robbery wasn't actually in Blizzard Gap. It was all the way over in Millpond," Bobcat reminded everyone as they walked out of the diner.

"That's about as close as we get to crime these days," said Maris.

But then she stopped so quickly that Bobcat bumped right into her. "Oh, no!" she said. "What happened to my truck?"

CHAPTER 4

Stay Away from
Blizzard Mountain!

The red pickup truck was just where they had left it. But now it was tilted to one side, like a sinking ship.

"Look," said Henry. "Both tires on one side are flat."

"Great!" fumed Maris. "This is just great!"

"It'll be okay," said Jessie. "We can fix the tires."

"Better yet, I'll get Lulu the mechanic to come over from the gas station. She can patch and pump those tires in no time flat," Bobcat said.

"Oh, okay," Maris said grumpily.

While Bobcat was gone, the Aldens all examined the tires very carefully. But they couldn't find a nail or a piece of glass or anything that would have made a hole in the tires so they would go flat.

"Someone must have let the air out of the tires," said Henry at last.

"That's what I think," Maris agreed. She folded her arms. "If I didn't know better, I'd think someone was out to get me."

"But why would anyone do that?" asked Violet.

Just then, a big white tow truck pulled up. Lulu got out of the tow truck, along with Bobcat.

"Bad luck," said Lulu, raising her eyebrows. With that, she went to work pumping air back into the tires. "No leaks," Lulu reported when she finished. "Looks like someone played a mean trick on you, Maris, and just let the air out of those tires."

Maris sighed. "Let's get going," she said.

"Or we won't even be able to start today."

"I just hope we don't have any more bad luck," said Violet in a low voice.

Jessie frowned. "Bad luck? No. I think it's more than that. A dead battery. Two flat tires."

"And all that talk about ghosts on Blizzard Mountain," said Henry. "It's almost like someone doesn't want us to go to Blizzard Mountain."

"Is it a mystery?" asked Benny eagerly.

"It might be, Benny," said Henry. "It just might be a mountain of a mystery."

Bobcat had picked up his truck at the park ranger office in town. Now he led the way in his truck, while Maris and the Aldens followed. The narrow winding mountain roads seemed to get bumpier and narrower with each passing mile. At last they came to a bare patch of dirt along one side of the road. Bobcat pulled over. So did Maris.

"Where's the trail?" Benny asked.

"Right there," Maris said, pointing.

Benny squinted and frowned. He didn't see anything but trees.

They put on their packs and reknotted their hiking boots and they each took a drink of water. Then Maris led the way toward the trees. She stepped between two trees and over a small boulder, and there it was: a faint trail threading through the trees.

Jessie could see white blazes of paint on the trees before them now, marking the trail ahead.

"It's almost like a secret trail," said Violet.

"There's been a rough trail here ever since I can remember," Maris told them. She made a face. "People using it to look for Stagecoach George's treasure, I guess."

They were passing a spooky-looking group of twisted dead trees. Jessie couldn't help asking, "Has anybody else ever seen the ghost of Stagecoach George? Besides Chuck?"

"People *say* they have," said Maris.

"Like that couple that got lost on Blizzard Mountain a couple years back," Bobcat said. "When the rescue team found them, they both said they'd seen a ghost."

"They'd been lost in the woods for three long, cold days," said Maris. "They were so scared they thought *you* were a ghost at first. Ghosts don't exist, Bobcat. Keep that in mind."

"Some of the other rangers have seen and heard strange things in these mountains," Bobcat argued stubbornly.

"But not ghosts," said Maris.

"I'd like to see a ghost," said Benny. "Then we could catch it. And if it was Stagecoach George, we could make him help us find the treasure."

Maris looked over her shoulder in surprise at Benny. "You're not afraid of ghosts?"

"No!" said Benny. "Boo to ghosts!"

Everyone laughed.

"Well, I'm glad to hear it," said Bobcat. "It's always good to have brave company in the mountains."

They walked quietly after that. Bobcat pointed out red squirrels that dashed up trees as they went by. Jessie saw a crow flapping heavily through the branches above them. Something slid into a stream with a splash when the hikers scrambled across the rocks in the streambed.

After a while, Violet said, "It's so quiet. And empty!"

"Oh, animals are everywhere around us," Bobcat said. "They can see us. Hear us, too, probably from miles away."

"I haven't seen any animals except squirrels and crows," Benny said.

"But they see you," said Bobcat. "Right now, they're sitting back and saying, 'Now, who do you suppose that is, walking right through our front yard?'"

Jessie laughed. "We'll have to be good guests and not make a mess," she said.

"Right," Maris said over her shoulder.

They hiked, stopped for lunch by another stream, then hiked some more. It got later and later.

Benny's feet began to hurt.

Suddenly Henry said, "I see a house!"

"The lean-to," said Maris. "Good. We've got just enough daylight left to set up camp." She led the way off the trail to a rough low building that looked like half of a triangle made of logs. A slanted log roof and log walls ran down to meet a log floor on the sides and in the back. The open front of the lean-to faced a stone fire pit.

"We'll camp here tonight," said Maris.

"Do we put our tent inside?" asked Benny.

Bobcat laughed. "Nope. The only things you put inside are balsam tree branches. You put those on the floor and put your sleeping bags on top. I'm going to put my tent right over there, and I'm going to put balsam tree branches in it, too."

Henry shivered. "It's getting colder," he said. "Let's build a fire right away."

"We need to hurry," Maris said. "It's getting dark."

Quickly everyone went to work. Soon the lean-to was piled with soft, sweet-smelling balsam and a fire was roaring in front of the lean-to. They sat down on the edge of the lean-to in front of the fire and made a dinner of soup mix cooked with boiling water over the fire, cheese, fruit, and bars of chocolate for dessert.

After dinner, the Aldens and Bobcat set out to explore the woods around their campsite. They had gone a little way when suddenly Jessie held out her hand. "Look! It's snowing!" she cried.

"Time to get back to the lean-to," Henry said.

They hurried back to camp. As they got closer, they saw Maris standing at the edge of the light cast by the fire. She turned a big flashlight in their direction and said, "Bobcat? Is that you?"

"It's us," said Bobcat.

"What is it?" Jessie asked. "You look worried."

"We weren't lost," Benny said.

"It wasn't that." Maris smiled. "I thought I heard something."

Everyone stopped to listen. They heard wind whispering in the trees. They saw shadows made by the fire leap up in the darkness. They felt the cold touch of snow-flakes.

But nothing more.

At last Maris said, "It must have been an animal."

"That's about the only thing that would be up here," Bobcat said.

"True," said Maris. "Okay. Let's get some rest."

Maris banked the fire so it would stay hot through the night. Then everyone got into their sleeping bags on top of the sweet-smelling balsam branches.

The night grew still. Through sleepy eyes, Benny watched the snow falling through the dim firelight.

He was almost asleep when Violet sat straight up and cried, "What's that?"

CHAPTER 5

The Hungry Thief

Everyone woke up. Maris, Henry, and Jessie switched on their flashlights.

The beams poked holes in the darkness. But nobody saw anything.

"I heard someone walking!" Violet insisted. "Over there." She pointed.

Bobcat came around the side of the lean-to from his tent. "What's going on?" he asked.

"Violet heard someone," Henry told him. He pointed.

"I'll check on the food," Bobcat said. "Maybe that's what you heard, an animal doing a little grocery shopping."

They watched Bobcat's flashlight bob away from the lean-to. A few minutes later, he came back. "Nothing," he said.

"I *know* I heard something," Violet said.

"It must have been the wind," Maris told her. "Or some small animal."

Everyone lay back down. One by one, the campers began to fall asleep.

Until Violet sat up once more. "There it is again," she cried.

This time, Maris walked to the edge of the clearing and shone her flashlight beam into the darkness all around. Everything was still and quiet. Bobcat called from his tent, "Everything okay, Maris?"

"Okay, Bobcat," she called back. To Violet, she said, "Nothing's here. Or if it is, it's run away."

"I know I heard something," Violet repeated.

Jessie put her hand on Violet's arm. "It's

just some animal," she told her sister. "The animals won't hurt us."

"It didn't sound like an animal," Violet said. "It sounded big. Like someone walking."

"A deer, maybe," said Maris, yawning.

"Or a bear?" Benny asked.

"If it was a bear, it'd make a lot more noise. It's no bear," Maris told him. "Let's get some sleep."

Everyone lay back down again. This time, it took longer for them to fall asleep. But at last, only Violet was awake. She lay with her eyes wide open, listening hard. She listened and listened.

But the woods were silent except for the creak of branches in the cold wind.

Then she heard a sound. She sat up, but she didn't say anything. She strained to hear.

The sound stopped. Violet began to relax. She lay back down. *Just a raccoon or something*, she told herself sleepily.

At last she fell asleep.

* * *

"Oh, great! That's just great!"

Bobcat was shouting. Violet sat up and blinked. A thin frosting of snow decorated everything. Tracks made patterns in the snow.

Maris stood by the warm fire heating a pan of water. "What is it, Bobcat?" Maris called.

A moment later, Bobcat came into sight. His hair was wild and he looked upset and angry.

Benny and Henry were right behind him. "It was a bear!" Benny said gleefully, before Bobcat could answer Maris.

Jessie came trotting around the other corner of the lean-to, holding her toothbrush. "Where's a bear?" she asked.

But Bobcat was shaking his head. "If it was a bear, I'll eat my hat," he said. "No bear is that neat."

"Did something eat the food?" asked Maris.

"You guessed it," Bobcat said. "About half of it is gone. Clean gone. No broken-open packets of soup, no dried noodles scattered on the ground. Just gone."

Maris frowned. "That doesn't sound like a bear."

"Did you see any footprints in the snow?" Jessie asked.

"No," said Henry. "It must have happened early in the night, when the snow had just started to fall."

"Maybe we should just give up and start over," Bobcat said.

"We have food left, don't we?" Maris asked.

"Some — " Bobcat held up a small bag of sugar. "Powdered milk. Sugar. Some dried beans. About half a dozen chocolate bars. The peanut butter sandwiches. Oh, yeah, and some dried oatmeal."

Maris made a face. "It could be worse," she said.

Jessie looked at her sister. "You were right, Violet. You did hear something!"

Maris sighed. "Well, whoever did this left us enough food for today. If we can get more supplies, we should be fine."

Now Bobcat sighed. "I'll do it," he volunteered. "I'll go back to Blizzard Gap and get more food and meet you at the next campsite."

"Can you make it all the way down and back up to the old cabin by tonight?" Maris asked.

"If I start now," Bobcat answered.

"I could come with you," Henry offered. "I can carry some of the supplies."

Bobcat shook his head. "Stay here and help with the trail," he told Henry. "I'm used to carrying a heavy backpack. It won't be a problem."

A few minutes later, as the Aldens and Maris packed up the camp, Bobcat put on his almost-empty backpack. "When you see me again," he said, "this pack will be full of groceries."

With a wave and a smile, Bobcat headed back down the trail. Soon after, the Aldens and Maris had the campsite as clean as if they'd never been there. Then they, too, put on their packs and headed in the opposite direction.

They didn't walk fast. Maris stopped to make marks on trees with paint and write notes in a small notebook. Sometimes she took photographs or drew diagrams. The snow stayed on the ground in the shade but began to melt along the trail. Their boots made wet, squishing sounds as the Aldens walked.

Maris showed them the neat, even tracks of a fox where it had crossed the trail.

"What's this?" asked Violet, pointing to another set of tracks.

"Rabbit," said Maris. "And one with a sore foot, from the looks of it."

"How can you tell?" asked Jessie.

"Look at this footprint. The other three tracks are deep. But the right front one is blurred and only deep at the toes, as if the rabbit put its foot down quickly, then lifted it up again, dragging it a little."

"Oh," said Jessie. "I see."

They hiked on. At last, when the sun was high overhead, Maris said, "It's lunchtime. Why don't you rest here? I'm going to look around and see if I can find a way

around these rocks that isn't so steep."

Benny and Jessie sat on a log. Violet found a spot on a rock in the sun. Henry spread his waterproof jacket out on a patch of leaves and sat on that. They ate peanut butter sandwiches they'd made the day before and drank water that Maris had filtered from a stream that morning. For dessert they each had a chocolate bar.

"If it wasn't a bear, I wonder who took our food last night," Henry said.

"Half our food," said Jessie. "Whoever it was left us some food so we wouldn't starve."

"A sort of nice thief," said Violet.

"Maybe it was the thief who stole all that stuff from the museum," Benny said.

"I don't think so," said Henry. "That thief would be long gone by now. But I do think it was a person, not a bear. If a bear had torn down our food bag, it would have left a big mess. There wasn't a mess. I mean, the bag had burst open, but only some of the stuff had been taken."

"The chocolate bars weren't taken," said

Jessie. "If I was a bear, I'd take *all* the chocolate bars first."

Everyone nodded. Then Violet said, thoughtfully, "It's almost as if someone were trying to scare us off, but they wanted to make sure we didn't go hungry getting back home."

"You're right," agreed Henry. "I don't think a bear would be that thoughtful."

"Then who was it?" Benny asked. He looked around. "Is someone following us?"

Violet looked around, too. She shivered a little. "I hope no one is following us, Benny," she said.

"Lots of people knew we were coming up this way," Jessie said. "Carola. Rayanne."

"Chuck," said Benny.

"All the people in the coffee shop," said Violet.

"But who would want to follow us all the way up here and steal our food?" asked Henry. "And why?"

"Not Chuck. He's got crutches," Benny said.

"Rayanne?" asked Violet.

Jessie shook her head. "I don't think so. She was busy at work."

"That leaves Carola. She doesn't want us here," said Henry.

"She could have sneaked into town and let the air out of the tires," Jessie said. "And she could have fixed Maris's car so it wouldn't start yesterday morning."

"She said she had an appointment in Millpond," Henry said.

"She could have been making that up," Jessie said. "Just like she might have been pretending not to remember Maris had told her we were hiking up Blizzard Mountain today."

"Or if she did have to go to Millpond, maybe someone's helping her," said Violet. "She fixed Maris's battery, but someone else let the air out of the tires and stole the food."

"Who?" Benny wanted to know.

They were silent for a moment. Then Henry said slowly, "It could be Bobcat."

"I like Bobcat!" Benny said indignantly.

"We all do. But he might not want people up here, either, Benny. Just like Carola," Henry said. "They could be working together."

"He was in his tent last night," said Jessie. She thought for a moment, then added, "Both times Violet heard the noise, Bobcat didn't come check on it or say anything until after the noise had stopped. So maybe he wasn't in the tent at all."

"Maybe he was being a bear," said Violet.

"It would have been easy for him to have let the air out of the tires while he was doing his errands," Henry said.

"That's right. He did other errands before he came to the diner. He could have done it then," Violet recalled.

"It wasn't Bobcat!" Benny said, sounding almost angry.

"Maybe not, Benny. I hope not," Henry said. "But — "

He didn't have a chance to say more. Maris came through the woods toward them. "Let's go," she said. "I think I've found a nice little detour around these rocks."

The Aldens jumped up and shouldered their packs. Before they left, Maris made a mark on a tree, with an arrow beneath it. "So Bobcat can find us," she said, "when he comes up the trail this afternoon."

The Aldens all looked at one another. They didn't say anything. But they were all wondering the same thing.

What if Bobcat didn't come back at all?

CHAPTER 6

A Haunted Cabin?

Late that afternoon, Violet stopped. "Look!" she said.

Through the trees, they saw an old cabin.

"That's it," Maris said. "We're here." She turned off the narrow, almost invisible path she'd been following and marking, and pushed her way through the bushes.

"Too bad old Chuck didn't know about this cabin when he broke his ankle," she said as she led the way to the cabin. "He was just down the trail. He was in his tent and snug enough. But he'd have been much more comfortable in the old cabin."

The cabin sat on a small patch of level ground, its back almost against the side of the mountain. Wooden shutters were closed tightly against the one window, but the door sagged a little and piles of leaves, branches, and straw seemed to be about to crash down on them from the roof as they got closer.

"It looks like a *haunted* cabin," said Benny.

"Not haunted. Just not used in a while. Bobcat and I did a few repairs a while back, but we haven't been here in a long time."

She pushed open the door of the cabin and led the way inside. Clouds of dust rose around her feet.

She sneezed. "Whew!" she said. "I don't remember it being this dirty when I left. It's almost like someone dumped a bucket of dirt in here."

"We can clean it up," Violet said. "Don't worry."

They dropped their packs on the rough bunk beds built along one wall. Maris put hers on the floor near the old woodstove.

Benny found a rusty basin with a bucket next to it on a shelf beneath one of the two shuttered windows. "Is this for water?" he asked.

"For washing dishes and your face," said Maris. "It's the cabin sink."

A rickety table and some stools stood near the stove. On the wall above the rusty basin was a small white metal cabinet. Beneath it, a row of tin cups hung from hooks.

"Let's get some wood for the stove," Henry said.

"Good idea," agreed Maris. "Then we can have a nice fire going to cook our food when Bobcat gets here in a little while."

But although they kept the fire hot, the sun went down and no Bobcat showed up.

"Maybe he's lost," said Benny, looking worried.

"Not Bobcat," said Maris. "He's too good a woodsman for that. He probably didn't make it down the trail in time to come back up tonight. I bet he's camped at the lean-to. He'll be here tomorrow."

No one said anything. Everyone wanted to believe that Bobcat was on his way, but none of the Aldens could be sure of that.

At last Violet said in a small voice, "What do we do about dinner?"

"Well, we've got some oatmeal, don't forget," said Maris cheerfully. "And I've got a few things in my tin cabinet over there."

She walked over to the cabinet. She peered inside. "We have a big metal canister of dried beans," she reported. "And some rice in this metal box. And I think . . . yes. Two packages of macaroni and cheese in this metal box. And a can of tomatoes! I'd forgotten about that!"

"Why is everything in metal boxes?" Benny wanted to know.

"This is my pest-proof food cabinet," Maris explained. "I lugged it all the way up here when I first laid out the trail this summer. It's metal to keep out mice, raccoons, chipmunks, and rodents. Everything inside is in metal, too, to help keep the smells inside the cabinet. That keeps any hungry bears away. If a bear can't smell anything inside, it's not going to bother."

"Wow," said Benny.

"We can make stew for dinner," Violet said. "Bean and tomato stew. With rice."

"Good idea," said Henry. He was hungry.

"Let's get to work," said Jessie.

When they had finished dinner, they settled into the bunk beds. The cabin was rough, but they were glad to be indoors. After their long hike, they had no trouble falling asleep.

They had leftover stew at lunch the next day. "And we'll have stew again tonight, too, if Bobcat doesn't get here soon," said Maris. She sounded worried.

"If Bobcat doesn't come, will we have to leave?" asked Violet.

"No," said Maris slowly. "We'll do fine on beans for another couple of days, which is how long I'd planned to be here. It's just that we're going to get mighty tired of beans."

Benny didn't say anything. He liked most

food, but he was already getting tired of beans for every meal!

After lunch, they walked farther up the mountain, helping Maris clear a section of trail. They cut back bushes and cleared away fallen trees. It was hard work.

Late in the afternoon, they returned to the cabin.

They saw no sign of Bobcat.

Maris shook her head. "If he doesn't come tomorrow, maybe I'll hike back down the trail to make sure he hasn't fallen or gotten hurt on his way up here," she said.

"What if he has?" Violet said, sounding more worried than Maris.

"Bobcat can take care of himself," Maris said. "Don't worry. He's trained in wilderness emergency rescue, just like all the park rangers are."

"Oh," said Violet.

"I'm hot," Benny announced.

"Me, too," said Jessie in surprise. "I can't believe how hot I am. Especially since it snowed the night before last."

"Hard work and sunshine," said Maris with a smile. "Why don't we head down to that stream over there and stick our feet in the water? That should cool us off."

At once the Aldens jumped up and headed for the stream. They lined their boots behind a log at the top of the little bank above the stream, then slipped and scrambled down to the water.

"It's freezing!" Violet squealed.

"It's so cold it makes my teeth hurt," said Benny, dipping one toe in and then the other.

They stood on the rocks in the warm sun and played in the water, being careful not to get anything more than their toes wet. Maris sat nearby, laughing. She splashed cold water on her face and lifted it to the sun. "This is one of the reasons I like working in this park," she said.

"I'm going to be a park ranger when I grow up," Benny said. "And a detective."

"Oh, Benny," said Violet.

They skipped stones on the water and made boats out of leaves that they sent

swirling downstream. Violet gathered a collection of pretty colored rocks from the stream.

"Look!" said Benny suddenly. "Gold!" He held out a sparkling rock. They all came to peer at it.

"I'm afraid not, Benny," said Maris. "Those sparkling chips are mica, not gold."

"It's pretty anyway," said Violet.

"Here. You can have it for your rock collection," said Benny generously.

"That's nice of you," Maris said. "And I have something you can add to your collection."

"What collection?" Benny asked, puzzled.

"Your collection of knowledge," Maris said teasingly. She bent over and showed the Aldens a small plant with waxy round leaves. It grew close to the earth. Maris broke off a leaf and rubbed it between her fingers. "Smell," she said.

Violet took a cautious sniff. "Peppermint?" she asked.

"Nooo," said Jessie.

"Gum. It smells like chewing gum," Benny said.

"It does, sort of," Henry agreed.

"You're all close. It's wintergreen," said Maris. "Just like in wintergreen gum. You can chew on it or use it to make tea out here in the woods."

"Wow," said Benny. He stuffed a leaf in his mouth and blinked in surprise at how strong the flavor was.

Maris looked at the sky. "It's getting dark. Time to get back," she said.

One by one, the Aldens scrambled up the side of the stream bank to where their hiking boots waited by the log.

And then Henry said, "Oh, no!"

"What is it, Henry?" asked Violet.

"My hiking boots!" said Henry. "They're gone!"

"Gone?" Jessie looked around. "Are you sure?"

"They were right here with everybody else's," Henry said. He pointed. "Now they're not."

"Uh-oh," said Benny. His eyes widened. "It's Stagecoach George. He's been here."

"No ghost did this," said Maris.

"Maybe it was an animal," suggested Violet.

"I guess it could be," Maris said. "But it doesn't make sense. Why would an animal take a pair of boots? *One* boot, maybe. Animals might make a meal on the leather. But a pair of boots?"

Henry said, "My feet are cold."

"Of course they are," said Maris. "Come on, Henry. Let's get back up to the cabin. You can put on a pair of wool socks. You do have extra socks, don't you?"

"I do," said Henry, looking a little more cheerful.

"We'll stay here and look around for the boots," said Jessie.

After Henry and Maris had gone, Benny, Violet, and Jessie scouted for Henry's missing boots. But they didn't find the boots, or even a clue about what had happened to them.

"I don't understand," Violet said as they walked back up to the cabin. "Do you think it's the same person who took our food?"

"It could be," Jessie said. She looked

around. "Or maybe it is an animal."

"A raccoon wearing Henry's boots," said Benny. He laughed at the idea.

Jessie smiled. But she knew that a raccoon hadn't stolen Henry's boots.

Henry stayed in the cabin the rest of the afternoon. "I'll cook dinner, since I can't hike," he said.

"I'll help," said Benny loyally.

"We'll do a little more work outside," said Maris. "And keep an eye out for Bobcat."

But once again, by suppertime no Bobcat had appeared.

No boots, either.

And their troubles were just beginning.

In the middle of the night, Violet sat up. "What was that?" she whispered.

No one answered. Everyone else was asleep.

Violet heard it again. A faint tap-tap-tapping.

Her fingers tightened on her sleeping bag. "Who's there?" she said in a louder voice.

Tap. Tap. Tap.

It was coming from outside the cabin.

Someone was tapping on the cabin wall!

Quietly, carefully, Violet leaned over and poked Jessie in the next bunk.

"Umpf," mumbled Jessie.

Violet poked her again.

"What?" said Jessie hoarsely.

"Shhh," Violet warned. "Listen."

Tap. Tap. Tap.

Now the sound was coming from across the cabin.

"Do you hear that?" Violet whispered.

"I hear it," Jessie said in a low voice.

Tap.

Tap.

Whatever it was sounded as if it was walking around the cabin.

Suddenly Benny said, "Violet?"

"Shhh," warned Violet.

Tap. Taptaptap.

The sound grew louder.

"It's the ghost!" cried Benny. "It's the ghost of Stagecoach George!"

He tumbled out of his bed and hurled

himself toward the cabin door. It was very dark, but Violet could just see Benny's shape in the dim light from the glowing stove.

"Benny, wait," hissed Jessie.

"W-what?" said Henry, waking from a deep sleep.

"What is it?" Now Maris was awake, too.

Benny didn't answer. He had his flashlight out. He threw the door open and raced into the night.

"Benny!" shouted Violet. Grabbing her own flashlight, she raced after him. Jessie was close behind.

"What's going on?" Maris said.

Violet stumbled out into the night. She saw the beam of Benny's flashlight disappear around the corner of the cabin.

She switched her own flashlight on and followed.

"Violet? Benny?" Jessie called behind her.

"This way!" Violet called back.

She rounded the side of the cabin.

"Benny!" she gasped.

But Benny had disappeared.

CHAPTER 7

Tap, Tap, Tap

"Benny!" shouted Violet.

Jessie ran up to her. "Where's Benny?" she asked.

"Help," squeaked a little voice from nearby. "Help! Help!"

"It's Benny," gasped Violet.

"Help!" Benny called again.

"Benny? Where are you?" Violet called.

"Over here!" Benny said.

They scrambled down through the bushes and tumbled out onto the Blizzard

Trail near the cabin. Benny was sitting in the middle of the trail.

"Oh, good," he said. "There you are! I was afraid you were lost."

"We weren't lost! We thought *you* were!" said Jessie indignantly.

"No," said Benny. "I dropped my flashlight and it went out. Or I might have caught the ghost."

Maris burst out of the bushes behind them and skidded to a stop. "Benny! Violet! Jessie! What on earth is going on?"

"Here's your flashlight, Benny," said Violet. She reached over and picked it up. "But I think it's broken."

"Is everybody all right?" Henry shouted from the door of the cabin. They could see him against the light from the stove inside. He was holding a flashlight, too, waving it back and forth like a search-light.

"We're fine!" Maris called. "We're on our way back." To Benny she said, "Are you hurt?"

"Nope," said Benny. He jumped to his feet. "I almost caught the ghost!"

"Ghost! I don't want to hear it. At least, not until we get back to the cabin. Then you can tell me what happened," Maris said.

They went back to the cabin. Henry had put another log on the fire and it was warm inside. Everyone sat down, and Violet and Benny told about the tapping sound on the cabin wall.

"Tapping?" Maris repeated. "That was no ghost. It was a tree. A branch."

"I don't think it was," Jessie said.

"Me either," said Violet.

"It sounded like a person," said Benny. "Or the ghost of a person. Like this." He leaned over and tapped on the cabin wall. "Only it came from outside."

"And it moved around the cabin, like someone was circling us, tapping on the walls," said Jessie.

"And then when I ran out, I saw something run into the woods. Toward the trail. But I tripped and dropped my flashlight and everything got dark, so I stopped chasing it," Benny added.

"You saw a ghost, Benny?" asked Henry.

"Well . . . no . . ." Benny admitted. "But I did see something run into the woods."

Maris pressed her hand to her forehead. "I don't believe this," she said, almost to herself. "Why would anyone be out here in the middle of nowhere, tapping on the cabin walls?"

"I don't know, but whoever or whatever it was, I bet you all scared them away," said Henry.

"Maybe it was whoever took your boots," said Benny. He paused. "Except I don't think a ghost would come out during the day to take someone's old boots."

"No, no, no," said Maris. "Stolen boots, ghosts tapping on walls. What is going on? If I didn't know better, I'd say this mountain really was haunted."

No one spoke for a long minute. Then Jessie said, "Haunted, or maybe someone who doesn't want us here is trying to scare us away."

"But why?" said Maris.

"Carola doesn't want a trail up here," Violet reminded Maris.

"Neither does Bobcat," Jessie added.

But Maris was shaking her head. "No!" she said again. "I don't believe Bobcat would do something like this. Or Carola, either."

"Both of them knew you were coming up here," Jessie argued. "Either one of them could have flattened your truck's tires out in front of the diner."

"And both of them are skilled enough to hike around in the woods, day or night, without getting lost," Henry said. "Carola could have followed us up here and taken our food. And my boots. And tapped on the walls."

"Or maybe Bobcat never really went back down the mountain," said Violet.

Henry took a deep breath. "Or there might be another reason that someone is trying to scare us away."

"Like what?" said Maris.

"Maybe someone has found Stagecoach

George's treasure," said Henry.

To Henry's surprise, Maris suddenly laughed. "No one's ever going to find that treasure, Henry, even if it does exist. People have been looking for years," Maris said. "Enough mysteries, okay? Let's get to sleep. We've got lots of work to do in the morning."

"But — " Benny began.

"No," said Maris firmly. "Not another word about ghosts or mysteries or treasure or anything else."

So Benny kept quiet. But he knew that all the Aldens would get up extra early in the morning to look for clues.

Even though they got up at sunrise, the Boxcar Children didn't find a single clue.

"Those smudges in the mud behind the cabin here *could* be footprints," Jessie said. She sighed. "And we could have made them ourselves in the dark."

"Do you really think someone could have found the hidden treasure?" asked Violet.

"I know someone is trying to scare us

away," Henry said. "I just don't know why."

Just then someone in front of the cabin shouted, "Wake up in there, you sleepy-heads!"

The Aldens hurried toward the sound of the voice. They found Carola and Rayanne standing in the clearing.

"Carola! Rayanne!" Jessie exclaimed. "What are *you* doing here?"

CHAPTER 8

Someone's Out There!

Carola looked surprised. "Hiking," she answered. "What does it look like?"

"I thought you didn't like hiking," Violet said to Rayanne.

Rayanne struggled out of her backpack. "Did I say that?" she said. "Well, when Carola told me she was going to hike up this way, I thought I'd give it a try." She made a face. "But this new backpack I bought is a pain. And so are these shoes."

"Once they're broken in, they'll feel better," said Carola. A sudden smile creased her face. "It's the people with all the fancy new stuff that get lost up here. Someone sells them expensive new gear. Tells them it'll be sure to make them into real wilderness wonders."

"Like that history teacher who broke his leg," added Rayanne.

"Chuck," said Benny.

"Him!" said Carola. "Ha. I've never met anybody who went hiking with so much new stuff and so little experience. It's a wonder he didn't get more lost!"

Rayanne said, "Well, sounds like he learned his lesson. He keeps warning people to stay away."

"And talking about ghosts. Ha!" said Carola. "Crazy talk, if you ask me."

Maris opened the cabin door. "Carola and Rayanne! Hi," she said. "If you've got any extra coffee and are willing to share, we'll provide the hot water."

"Sure," said Carola. "Didn't you bring enough coffee? I'm surprised at you, Maris."

"It got stolen," said Benny. "So did the rest of our food. *And* Henry's hiking boots."

"Did you see Bobcat on the trail?" asked Henry.

"Stolen? What? Did Bobcat steal your food and boots?" asked Rayanne, sounding bewildered.

"No, no, no. It's a long story," said Maris. "Come on in."

As Rayanne and Carola drank coffee, the Aldens ate their oatmeal and told the two newcomers everything that had been happening. When they'd finished, Carola said, "Could've been bears that took your food, but it doesn't sound right. It does sound like you've been having a blizzard of bad luck. But then, that goes with this mountain."

"Did you both just hike up the mountain?" asked Henry.

"Yep. Met Carola at the trailhead this morning, near where Maris's truck is parked. She waited until my days off at the diner so I could come with her," Rayanne told them.

"Have you seen any bears?" Violet asked. "We haven't."

Carola looked a little embarrassed. "No," she said shortly.

Everyone was quiet for a moment. Then Rayanne said to Maris, "Is there any reason someone would be out to get you?" she asked.

"No," said Maris firmly.

But Henry said, "We think someone might be trying to scare us away. Keep a trail from being built on Blizzard Mountain."

All four Aldens looked hard at Carola.

"Well, that's interesting," she said.

Rayanne asked, "Did you find any clues? Footprints, for example? You can tell a lot from footprints. The soles of shoes can tell you almost as much as someone's fingerprints, you know."

"No. No footprints," said Jessie regretfully.

Carola put down her coffee cup and stood up. "We'd better get a move on, Rayanne."

To Maris and the Aldens she said, "And we'll keep an eye out for anything suspicious. If someone is trying to scare you away and we find out anything, we'll let you know."

"Have a good hike," Maris said. "I'll walk you to the trail's edge." She and Rayanne headed toward the Blizzard Trail.

Carola stopped at the door to look back at the Aldens.

"If someone is trying to scare you off this mountain, maybe you should leave," she said. "I know I would."

Then she was gone, too.

"Wow," said Henry. "Do you think that was a warning?"

"A warning," said Jessie solemnly, "or a threat."

"Then Carola is the one who's trying to scare us off the mountain?" asked Violet.

"I'm not sure. She could be," said Jessie.

"But she just hiked up here with Rayanne," said Benny.

"That's what she said, Benny. She could have been following us, though. And then hiked *down* to meet Rayanne this morning," Jessie said.

"Unless it's Bobcat who's been trying to scare us," said Henry.

"Or maybe Bobcat and Carola are working together," said Jessie.

"What about Rayanne?" Violet suggested. "She asked a lot of questions."

Benny nodded. "She sounded like one of us. Like a detective."

"I wonder why she's up here. She doesn't even like mountains, remember?" said Henry.

"Maybe she's pretending she doesn't like mountains," Violet said.

"I guess it's possible, Violet," Henry said.

Benny said, "I think it's the treasure. The ghost is trying to keep us away from it."

Henry frowned. "There's no such thing as ghosts," Henry said. "But you might have a point."

"You think it's Stagecoach George, too?" Benny asked, looking very surprised.

Jessie and Violet looked startled, too.

"Maybe not a ghost," said Henry. "But

what if someone has found the treasure, or a clue to the treasure? Maybe it's not a ghost, but a person trying to keep us away."

Jessie's eyes sparkled with sudden excitement. "Maybe you're right, Henry! Remember, in the diner people talked about hikers coming up here to look for the lost treasure. What if someone has found it?"

"But why haven't they taken it?" asked Violet.

"Because it's so heavy. Gold is heavy. Maybe they found it and now they have to come back to get it," said Jessie.

Just then, Maris came back. "Let's get to work," she said. "I think this weather could turn bad any day now. We need to get finished up here and get back down the mountain."

As she walked away, Jessie said to the others, "Maybe we shouldn't tell Maris about what we talked about. We don't want to worry her until we've figured out the mystery."

"Oh," Benny said. "Okay."

"Who's going to help me on the trail?" Maris called.

"I will," said Jessie.

"Since I don't have any shoes, I guess I'll work around the cabin," said Henry.

"Benny and I will stay with you, Henry," said Violet. "And keep you company."

"And look for treasure," said Benny under his breath.

But by late afternoon, the only treasure that had been found was a penny wedged in the floorboards of the cabin and a scrap of purple cloth caught on a splinter of wood near the cabin door. Violet tucked the scrap of purple in her backpack to keep as a souvenir of the trip and Benny put the penny in his pocket.

When Jessie and Maris returned, they were both dusted with snow. Violet showed them the scrap of purple cloth she'd found and Benny told them about his new penny.

Then Jessie said, "I found something, too." She reached in her pocket and pulled out a handful of small, shiny green leaves.

Benny knew what it was at once. "Wintergreen!" he said.

Maris smiled and said, "Right, Benny. We thought we'd use it to make some hot tea to go with dinner."

"Dinner," said Benny at once. "Good!"

After dinner and hot tea, Maris checked to make sure the cabin was locked up tight, windows and doors. Then it was time for bed.

In no time every one of the Aldens had scrambled into a sleeping bag. "I'm going to sleep like a log," Jessie announced.

No one answered. Everyone had fallen fast asleep, just like that.

And a moment later, Jessie did, too.

But no one slept like a log that night.

"OOOOOOOOOOOOOOH!" Something wailed right outside the cabin wall.

Jessie bolted up.

"OOOOOOOOOOOOOH!"

"Hey! What's that?" Benny said.

Across the room, Maris called out, "Is everyone okay?"

"OOOOOOOOOOOOOOH!" The sound

came from the other side of the cabin now.

"The ghost!" cried Benny, sounding scared and excited at the same time.

"A screech owl," said Maris. But her voice was uncertain.

She scrambled out of her sleeping bag and lit one of the candles inside its glass lantern on the table.

Jessie had on one boot and was pulling the other on. Violet was sitting up in her sleeping bag, her eyes wide. Henry was struggling to pull on his thick wool socks.

"OOOOOOOH." The sound came from the back of the cabin. But this time it wasn't so loud. It sounded as if it were fading away.

"That's no screech owl," Jessie said.

"Let's go out there! I want to catch the ghost," Benny said excitedly.

Jessie grabbed her flashlight. "We all do, Benny," she said. "But you can't catch anything but a cold if you go outside in the snow without shoes or a coat."

"Oh, all right," Benny said.

He ran back to his bunk and stuffed his

feet into his boots. By the time he had his coat on, everyone was ready and had their flashlights on. The Aldens raced out of the cabin door into the dark and snowy night.

"Look! Tracks in the snow," said Violet.

They followed the scramble of tracks around the cabin and all over the clearing as well as they could.

Suddenly Jessie pointed. "That way! The tracks go that way!" she said.

Being careful not to step on the tracks, the Aldens followed the tracks to the stream.

"I think I see more tracks on the other side. I'll check," said Jessie. She scrambled nimbly across the rocks while the others waited and watched.

Henry danced from one foot to the other. He could feel the cold snow through his socks. He didn't dare try to follow the others across the icy-cold stream.

How would he ever get back down the trail?

"The tracks stop here," Jessie called from the other side of the water.

"No more tracks?" Henry called back.

"Nope. It's like whoever it was just disappeared," Jessie reported.

Benny nodded wisely. "Ghosts can do that," he said. "Stagecoach George probably just flew away."

"Ghosts don't leave footprints," argued Violet. But she looked around nervously.

Maris shivered. "I agree. Even if there was such a thing as a ghost, no ghost made these tracks. Look at them."

Five flashlights pointed down on the footprints. They were large and deep and smudged along one side.

"Something heavy, with big feet," said Violet, remembering some of the tracking lessons Maris had given them.

"Right, Violet," Maris said. "Heavy weight makes deep tracks. And big footprints mean big feet, which usually means a big person."

Maris knelt and studied the prints some more. "Expensive hiking boots, but not brand-new," she reported. "Someone's been hiking in these for a long time."

"Maybe it's someone small wearing big boots," said Jessie. "Someone small in disguise."

"And it looks like whoever it is might be carrying something heavy," Henry said, forgetting about his own cold, bootless feet for a moment.

"Why?" asked Benny.

"Because the track is uneven," Henry pointed out. "See how it is smudged and blurred on the left side?"

"Another good observation," Maris said. "Someone who's going to be sneaking around in the wilderness in the middle of the night could be carrying a heavy pack with emergency supplies in it."

"And it's either packed unevenly, or somehow it got thrown off balance," Jessie said.

"Right again," said Maris. Suddenly she shivered. "But let's get back inside. I'm getting cold."

Reluctantly, the Aldens returned to the cabin. As they approached, Henry swung his flashlight around the clearing. "The footprints lead into the clearing from the trail," he noted. "And away from the clearing across the stream. And then they stop. How did he — or she — do that?"

"I know!" exclaimed Jessie. "Maybe the person walked backward in his own steps to the stream and then walked up the stream."

"Good idea, Jessie," Maris said. "We'll check around farther up and downstream tomorrow."

"If the snow hasn't covered the tracks," Henry said. "Or — "

But Henry didn't finish what he was about to say. Violet's flashlight beam had stopped on the roof of the cabin.

"Look at that!" Jessie exclaimed.

Henry just stared. He couldn't believe his eyes!

CHAPTER 9

We'll Be Coming Down the Mountain

"Your boots!" shouted Benny. "Look!"

Henry's brown hiking boots were sitting on the cabin roof, right above the door!

Henry walked up to the cabin and stepped onto a stump next to the cabin door. He reached up and took down the boots.

"These are my boots for sure," he said. "And I don't think they've been here long. There's hardly any snow on them."

"But where did they come from?" Violet cried.

"Maybe it's a joke," Benny said.

"I don't think so, Benny," said Henry. "And I don't think it was a ghost."

"Do you think it was whoever was making all that noise?" asked Violet.

"It had to be," said Jessie. She frowned. "But why? Why would anyone take your boots and then bring them back?"

"Maybe the thief realized that Henry couldn't hike back down without his boots," said Benny.

"Oh, no!" gasped Violet. "What if the boot thief took something else?"

They all pushed quickly into the cabin. But nothing had been touched. The cabin was just as they had left it.

"I don't care who took the boots! I've had it," Maris declared. "We're going home tomorrow."

"But what about the trail?" asked Jessie.

"We've done as much on the trail as we need to do before the winter snow sets in. And from the looks of things, if we don't head down the trail soon, winter could trap us here," said Maris.

"But we haven't caught the ghost . . . or the thief yet," said Benny.

"We will," said Jessie.

Maris woke the Aldens before the sun was up the next morning. "It looks like it has been snowing off and on all night," she told them. "We need to get down the mountain while we can."

They ate quickly, then loaded their packs and headed out.

"All the footprints from last night are gone," said Benny.

"Yep. Whoever's been bothering us got lucky," said Henry.

The snow fell and fell as the little group slipped and slid down the side of the mountain. Drifts of snow soon covered the trail and Maris stopped often to make sure that they hadn't lost their way.

Halfway down, Benny sank onto a rock. "My legs are *tired*," he said. "They don't want to walk anymore."

"I could carry you," Henry said.

But Maris shook her head. "Benny's too

heavy for you to carry on this slippery trail," she said. As she spoke, she pulled out the lightweight ax she carried and began to hack at a small tree by the trail.

"What are you doing?" Jessie asked.

"Building a sort of sled to pull Benny on," Maris said. Swiftly she cut another tree. "Trim the branches off that tree and I'll trim this one."

When the branches were trimmed off both trees, Maris cut one trunk exactly in half. Then she cut the other trunk into four pieces. She laid the two long pieces of wood side by side. She tied the four shorter pieces across the two long pieces, in the middle.

"It looks like a ladder," said Benny.

"It does," said Maris. "But it's your new sled."

Quickly Maris wove some of the branches in and out of the rungs of the ladder-sled. Last of all, she lashed her waterproof tarp over the branches.

"Hop on," she told Benny. "And let's go."

Benny climbed onto the sled and grabbed each side. Maris picked up the two poles on the end of the sled facing down the trail and started forward.

"Hold on tight," she said. Benny and the sled slid over the snow.

Henry and Maris took turns pulling Benny. With Benny in the sled, they could all travel much faster.

They reached the bottom of the trail in the late afternoon. They were all very tired.

"Looks like we're the last ones out," said Maris. "Carola's truck is gone and so's Ray-anne's car. They must have come out even earlier than we did. I guess the snow buried their footprints."

"Bobcat's truck is gone, too," said Violet.

"At least we know he's not up on the mountain somewhere," said Jessie.

"We'll check in town," said Maris. "I'm sure Bobcat is fine and there's a logical reason why he didn't come back."

"Whew," said Henry, helping Benny climb off the sled. "I was getting worried for a while there that we were going to get stuck on Blizzard Mountain."

"It's a good thing you built me a sled," said Benny to Maris. "Thank you."

"You're welcome, Benny," said Maris. "It's a good way to move something heavy, isn't it? Especially when it snows."

"Sort of like a dogsled," said Jessie.

"Yes," agreed Maris. She smiled tiredly. "It's also a good thing you got your boots back, though, Henry. You would have been a lot heavier to pull!"

They climbed into the truck.

"I'm hungry," Benny announced.

Maris nodded. "Next stop, the diner," she said. "We can get something to eat. And we can ask about Bobcat."

Benny pushed the diner door open. "It smells good!" he said. He raced to the counter to sit down.

"Rayanne!" said Jessie in surprise, as she and the others followed Benny. "Did you hike down Blizzard Mountain this morning and then come to work?"

The silver-haired waitress shook her head. "Nope. We hiked back down last night. Carola didn't like the way the weather looked. Hiking at night. Ha!"

"I guess you didn't like it," said Benny.

"You guessed that right," said the waitress. "What can I get you?"

"Anything but beans," said Benny.

"Has anyone seen Bobcat?" Maris asked abruptly.

"I haven't," said Rayanne. "No one I've talked to has."

"I'm going to go check at the general store and see what I can find out," said Maris. She slid off her counter stool and walked briskly out.

Jessie fixed Rayanne with a solemn look. "You hiked down the mountain last night?" she asked.

"If I go hiking again, it's going to be in the summer," declared Rayanne.

"Next time, you can take that purple opera cape," said Benny.

"What did you say?" Jessie asked.

"Remember that old purple velvet opera cape that got stolen?" he said. "And people were talking about it here and joking that you could use it to fly down the mountain like a superhero?" Benny flapped his arms. "I just remembered that!" He laughed.

"That's it," Jessie whispered. "That's it!"

"What?" asked Violet.

But before Jessie could answer, the door to the diner opened.

Chuck limped in on his crutches.

"You're back," he said to the Aldens. "Did you have a good trip? See any ghosts?"

"Yes," said Benny.

"No," said Henry firmly.

"Not exactly," Jessie added.

"Well, at least you didn't get trapped in all this snow," Chuck said. He bent and knocked snow from his boots. "But I guess a little snow won't hurt these old boots of mine."

"Maybe you should get new boots," said Benny, "to go with all your new hiking stuff."

"New hiking stuff?" Chuck looked at Benny.

"Carola told us when you got lost, it was

because you had all new stuff," Benny said.

Chuck laughed and said, "I think I know what Carola said, and she's right. New gear isn't what makes you a good hiker. You have to learn that, just like lessons in school."

Rayanne put a menu in front of Chuck. He glanced down, then glanced up again. "Where's your friend Bobcat?" he asked the Aldens.

"He's missing," said Jessie. She had a very odd expression on her face.

"Missing?" asked Chuck. He raised his eyebrows. "That's strange. I just saw him a couple of days ago."

"You did?" Violet said, her voice going up in surprise.

"Sure. Outside the general store. He was loading supplies into his truck. Said he was on his way back up the mountain to bring them to you," Chuck said.

"He never hiked back up to bring us those supplies," Henry said.

Chuck stroked his beard as if trying to remember something. Then he said, "You

know, now that I think about it, I did wonder why Bobcat did what he did."

"What did Bobcat do?" Violet asked.

"He drove in the wrong direction when
he left here," said Chuck. "The opposite direction from Blizzard Mountain."

Jessie jumped up. "Thanks," she said.
"Come on, everyone. We have to find
Maris." She raced out of the diner.

The other Aldens exchanged surprised
looks. Then they followed their sister. They
met Maris just outside the door. "Bobcat's
okay," Jessie said.

"What? How do you know that?" Maris
asked.

"How do you know?" asked Henry at the
same time.

"Jessie?" Violet said.

"Do you know where Bobcat is?" asked
Benny.

"Not exactly, but I'm sure he's okay.
Come on! And I have a plan to catch the
ghost that's been trying to scare us all off
Blizzard Mountain," Jessie said. "This is
what we need to do — and why."

*   *   *

The Aldens walked back into the diner a few minutes later. "Back so soon?" Rayanne asked.

"We're going to call Grandfather. He's at Maris's cabin. We hope he can drive into Blizzard Gap to meet us for dinner," explained Henry.

"The phone booth is in the hall. I'll be right back," said Maris.

The Aldens settled down at a table.

Chuck chewed the hamburger he had ordered. He nodded to the Aldens, then said, "Did you find Bobcat yet?"

"We will. Tomorrow," said Jessie. "But we can't look for him now. It's too dark."

"I'm sure he's okay," Chuck said. "Maybe he had an emergency and had to leave in a hurry."

"Yes. That's what probably happened," agreed Jessie. She turned to Violet and said in a loud voice, "Show me that piece of cloth you found at the cabin, Violet."

Violet reached into her pocket and pulled out the small scrap of purple cloth.

"Velvet," said Jessie. "Purple velvet."

"It looks old," said Benny.

"Probably been stuck up in the cabin for years," said Henry. He made sure the others in the diner could hear their conversation.

"Velvet's a funny thing to find in an old cabin in the woods, don't you think, Violet?" Jessie asked.

"You're right," said Violet.

"Maybe it's a clue," said Benny. "To buried treasure."

Rayanne was standing behind the counter, motionless. Her eyes were fixed on the scrap of velvet Violet held. "Where did you find that?" she demanded.

"Up at the cabin," said Violet. "Isn't it pretty?"

Rayanne came around the counter and snatched up the bit of velvet. She stared at it, then slapped it down on the table. She went back to work without another word.

But the Aldens felt her sharp eyes watching them.

Chuck dropped his hamburger and

ketchup splashed on his shirt. He grabbed a napkin and begin to poke at the stain.

"Yes, it is a clue," Benny said, in a louder voice than before. "I bet it's a clue to where Stagecoach George hid his treasure."

"In the cabin? Oh, Benny, do you think so?" said Violet.

"I do," said Benny.

"Well, we should go up there and look," said Henry. "Maybe Maris will take us up tomorrow."

Now Chuck dropped the napkin. He bent over to pick it up and straightened. He hit his head on the table. "Ow!" he said.

"Tomorrow. First thing. We go on a treasure hunt," said Jessie.

"But . . . but . . . what about Bobcat?" asked Chuck.

"We'll find the treasure. And maybe Bobcat, too," said Benny, smiling. "We're *very* good at finding things. Ask anybody back in Greenfield."

Maris came back into the diner. "Your grandfather's on his way," she said.

"Good," said Henry. "We can tell him about this clue we found."

Violet held up the piece of velvet and nodded. "And about the ghost and how he tried to scare us away and didn't," she said. "And about how we're going to hike right back up Blizzard Mountain to that cabin and look for treasure."

CHAPTER 10

How to Catch a Ghost

"I'm glad it stopped snowing," whispered Violet.

"Me, too. And when the sun comes up, it'll be warmer," said Jessie.

They were huddled in the little lean-to just off the Blizzard Trail. They'd been there since right before dawn. From where they sat, they could see the trail clearly.

"It didn't turn out to be much of a snowstorm after all," Benny complained.

"Shhh, everyone!" Henry warned.

After that, the Aldens were quiet.

"What if this doesn't work?" Violet said very, very softly.

"Maris is waiting just down the trail at the next big rock," Henry reminded her. "One way or another, our trap will work."

"Listen . . ." Benny said.

They all grew quiet now. And then they heard it. Something was scraping over snow. Someone was coming down the Blizzard Trail.

Crunch, crunch, crunch went the sound of boots on thin snow.

There was also the sound of something heavy being pulled over that same thin snow. *Swish, bump, bump, swish.*

A figure appeared through the trees. Everyone held their breath.

The figure leaned forward and pulled hard on a rope in one hand. A sled bumped along at the end of the rope. "Whoa," the figure commanded, and raised one foot awkwardly to slow down the sled.

"Let's go," said Jessie, and leaped to her feet and out of the lean-to.

The person saw the four Aldens running

through the trees and, yanking the sled hard, began to run, too.

"Stop!" cried Jessie.

"Stop, thief!" shouted Benny. Henry jumped forward — and landed right on the sled.

The sled tipped over. The person pulling the sled stumbled and fell, but tried to get up and run again.

But by this time Maris had stepped out into the middle of the trail.

"Give up, Chuck," said Henry. "We know all about the gold."

The man turned and pushed the hood of his jacket back. Chuck's face was red.

"What a dumb thing I did," he said, and sat down hard on a fallen tree trunk.

Jessie stepped forward and pulled back the tarp on the sled. Underneath was a lump, covered with purple velvet. Carefully, she and Violet lifted the velvet cape. Gold bars shone beneath it.

"Gold!" said Benny.

"It's the museum gold," said Violet.

"I . . . I . . . oh, no," moaned Chuck, and buried his face in his hands.

"Not exactly gold," said a new voice.

Maris and the Aldens looked up in surprise at the woman striding up the trail.

"Rayanne?" asked Maris. "What are *you* doing here?"

"Rayanne Adams, private detective, at your service," said Rayanne.

"But you work at the diner!" said Violet.

"That's because I was undercover. What better place to find out what's going on than at the town's only diner?" asked Rayanne. She stared at Chuck. "You ought to be ashamed of yourself, mister, robbing that museum."

"I didn't mean to." Chuck looked up. "I was just standing there, and no one was around, and I saw how easy it would be to take the gold that was on display. I put a piece of tape on the back door lock and just pushed the door open right after the museum closed. I wrapped the gold in that old purple cape and carried it out."

"You're a private detective?" Maris asked Rayanne.

Rayanne nodded. "My nephew runs the museum. I'm retired now, but I agreed to take this case to help him out."

"That's why you asked so many questions! And knew so much about the museum theft!" cried Jessie.

"Yep," said Rayanne. "And I had my suspicions about Mr. Chuck Larson here. But until you came along, I couldn't prove anything. How did you know to make a trap for him?"

"Two clues," said Henry. "Shoes and purple velvet. Chuck was acting like a hiker who didn't know anything. But he wore good old comfortable hiking boots. Boots that had been used a lot."

"And they were worn down on one side, like a man who'd been limping while wearing them," said Jessie. "That matched the boot prints we found in the snow. The prints weren't very clear, but they were clear enough to show us that whoever walked around our cabin limped on the same foot as Chuck. Only we didn't know *why* he'd be following us."

"We thought first he'd found Stagecoach George's treasure. It wasn't until you mentioned the cape from the museum was purple velvet and we remembered that scrap of purple cloth Violet had found that things began to make sense," said Henry.

"That purple velvet was an important clue," Rayanne agreed. "It got my attention. And it got Chuck's attention, too."

"That's when we knew for sure Chuck was faking it. That his ankle was not all that broken anymore," said Benny.

Henry looked at Chuck. "You're not even a history teacher, are you? It was all faked."

Chuck groaned. "No," he confessed. "I'm a mountain guide from out West. I came here just to hike."

"We should have known you were no beginner when we found you all snug in your tent when you were injured. Beginners usually wander off the trail. And they aren't so prepared," said Maris.

"I was hoping you wouldn't notice that," Chuck said. "Anyway, I'd carried the gold, wrapped in the cape, in my pack, about halfway down Blizzard Mountain when I slipped and broke my ankle." He made a face at the memory.

"I knew I was near the cabin — I'd used it on the way over the mountain the first time. So I managed to get there and bury the gold under the floor of the cabin and put the boards back down."

"That's why there was so much dirt on the floor," said Violet. "We figured that out, too."

He nodded. "I guess that's when a piece of purple velvet tore off that old cape. Anyway, I dragged myself back over to the trail so no one would know I'd been in the cabin. I had enough supplies to last awhile, and I knew I'd be okay, that someone would come along before long."

"You let the air out of our tires, too," Benny accused Chuck.

"Yes, it was me. When I went to the bathroom at the diner, I really sneaked out and did that. And I followed you up the trail and took part of your food," Chuck confessed. "I hoped that would scare you off, but it didn't. So I followed you to the cabin and tried to scare you away then."

"And you took my boots," said Henry.

"I did. But I gave them back!" said Chuck. "I couldn't let you try to hike down the mountain without them, any more than I could leave you without any food at all. I'm a mountain guide. I just couldn't do it."

"You're a better mountain guide than a thief," said Rayanne. "That wasn't even gold that you took."

Chuck sat up. "What?" he said.

"Iron bars painted to look like gold, for the mining display," said Rayanne. "That's all it is. Heavy and worthless. It's the cape the museum wants back. It's an important part of this park's history."

Chuck's mouth had fallen open. So had Benny's.

"N-not gold?" Chuck managed to stammer at last.

"Nope," said Rayanne. "So now that

we've got the cape back, the museum's going to let you go."

"You will?" said Chuck. He jumped to his feet. "Oh, thank you! I'll never, ever do something like that again. I've never done anything like that before. I know it was wrong. I've learned my lesson."

"Good," said Jessie. She almost felt sorry for Chuck.

"Thank you," Chuck cried again. "Thank you."

"Go on, then," said Rayanne. "We'll get this down the mountain."

Chuck looked around. Then, almost running, he headed down the mountain.

As the Aldens and Maris and Rayanne came out of the woods at the bottom of the Blizzard Trail, Grandfather Alden stepped out of a car parked near Maris's truck.

"Grandfather!" said Jessie. "We caught the thief."

"And Rayanne's a real live detective," said Benny.

Another person got out of the truck.

"Bobcat!" said Maris. "There you are. What happened?"

"We forgot to ask Chuck what he told you to make you leave town," said Henry.

"So you figured it out, huh?" Bobcat chuckled. He shook his head. "And I fell for it, too. Chuck met me outside the general store. Must have been waiting for me, I realize now. He gave me a message, said it had been left at the diner for me. That's not unusual. Everyone knows that the people at the diner can always find you. It's the way a small town works."

"What was the message?" asked Violet.

"My brother had an attack of appendicitis. It said please come at once. Chuck said he'd see that someone else took supplies to you, so I drove to the airport and flew halfway across the country. Boy, was my brother surprised to see me. We had a nice visit, though." Bobcat grinned. "That buzzard!"

"Bobcat called when he got back," Grandfather explained. "I told him what had been going on and we drove here."

"But what about when your truck

wouldn't start, Maris? Did Chuck do that, too?" asked Violet.

"Nope. My truck's just an old truck. But Chuck knew about the trouble I'd been having with it. Carola had stopped by the diner earlier on her way out of town and been talking about it. That's what gave him the idea to try to scare us off the trail until he could get back up there and haul the gold out," said Maris.

"And because his ankle was hurting, he waited until the first snow so it would be easy to pull the gold out by sled. Only it wasn't gold," Henry concluded.

"Chuck made a mistake," said Rayanne. "And he got caught. Bad luck for Chuck."

"He always said Blizzard Mountain was a bad luck mountain," Bobcat said. "Looks like it was — for him."

"But good luck for us," said Benny.

Everyone looked at Benny. "What do you mean, Benny?" asked Jessie.

"Well, Stagecoach George's gold is still up on Blizzard Mountain," Benny said. "So on our next visit, we can go back and find it!"

GERTRUDE CHANDLER WARNER discovered when she was teaching that many readers who like an exciting story could find no books that were both easy and fun to read. She decided to try to meet this need, and her first book, *The Boxcar Children*, quickly proved she had succeeded.

Miss Warner drew on her own experiences to write the mystery. As a child she spent hours watching trains go by on the tracks opposite her family home. She often dreamed about what it would be like to set up housekeeping in a caboose or freight car — the situation the Alden children find themselves in.

When Miss Warner received requests for more adventures involving Henry, Jessie, Violet, and Benny Alden, she began additional stories. In each, she chose a special setting and introduced unusual or eccentric characters who liked the unpredictable.

While the mystery element is central to each of Miss Warner's books, she never thought of them as strictly juvenile mysteries. She liked to stress the Aldens' independence and resourcefulness and their solid New England devotion to using up and making do. The Aldens go about most of their adventures with as little adult supervision as possible — something else that delights young readers.

Miss Warner lived in Putnam, Connecticut, until her death in 1979. During her lifetime, she received hundreds of letters from girls and boys telling her how much they liked her books.